THE WEE MOUSE
Who Was Afraid of the Dark

A Grosset & Dunlap **ALL ABOARD BOOK**®

To Martha Newell
and her long-ago music box
—M.L.

 Published by Grosset & Dunlap, Inc., which is a member of The Putnam & Grosset Group, New York. ALL ABOARD BOOKS is a trademark of Grosset & Dunlap, Inc. Reg. U.S. Pat. & Tm. Off. THE LITTLE ENGINE THAT COULD and engine design are trademarks of Platt & Munk, Publishers, a division of Grosset & Dunlap, Inc. GROSSET & DUNLAP is a trademark of Grosset & Dunlap, Inc. Published simultaneously in Canada. Printed in the U.S.A. Library of Congress Catalog Card Number: 89-82228 ISBN 0-448-40060-X
F G H I J

THE WEE MOUSE
Who Was Afraid
of the Dark
By Margo Lundell
Illustrated by Lucinda McQueen
Grosset & Dunlap, Publishers

The Mouse family was on their way home. They had spent a fine spring day going upstream to find fresh watercress. Now Mr. and Mrs. Mouse guided the rowboat back down the stream toward their little house.

Wee Mouse, whom they dearly loved, stared at the dark shadows. "Night is coming," she whispered with a shiver.

Later that evening the Mouse family ate a wonderful supper of watercress salad with buttermilk dressing. But Wee Mouse hugged a blanket while she ate her dinner.

"Why are you holding that blanket?" asked Father Mouse.

"Because it's night," Wee Mouse answered.

Her parents looked at each other in surprise. Their little one had never been afraid of night before.

As always Mr. Mouse read a story to Wee Mouse before she went to bed. But this time Wee Mouse didn't want the story to end.

"Now you must go to sleep," said Father Mouse.

"No, no! Don't go," Wee Mouse begged. "Read more."

When Mother Mouse put out the light, Wee Mouse started crying.

"It's too dark," she said. "I can't see."

"I'll leave the door open," said Mother Mouse gently. "The hall light is on. It won't be too dark."

The next night was no better. Wee Mouse thought a hawk was hiding under her bed.

When it was time to go to sleep, Wee Mouse leaped into bed so the hawk couldn't grab her leg.

Her mother and father said the hawk was only in her imagination, but Wee Mouse said the hawk was real and his name was Hunnible.

Once she was in bed, Wee Mouse called downstairs to her parents again and again.

"Mommy," she begged. "I need a glass of water."

"Daddy," she cried. "I hear something outside the window."

Mr. and Mrs. Mouse came every time Wee Mouse called, but it didn't seem to help.

The next evening Mr. and Mrs. Chipmunk stopped by to visit.

"Why is Wee Mouse carrying that blanket around?" asked Mr. Chipmunk.

Mrs. Mouse explained that their daughter was afraid of the dark.

"We are up half the night with her," said Mr. Mouse, "trying to get her back to sleep."

"There is only one answer," announced Mrs. Chipmunk. "You must let Wee Mouse sleep with you."

That night Wee Mouse was very happy. She snuggled down in the middle of her parents' big bed and went right to sleep.

But Mr. and Mrs. Mouse found themselves tossing and turning the whole night through.

When morning came Mrs. Mouse was weary.

Mr. Mouse yawned and said, "Wee Mouse moves around a lot in her sleep. I'm afraid she kicked me more than once."

Mrs. Mouse agreed. Sharing their bed with Wee Mouse was not the answer.

One warm evening Mrs. Sparrow stopped by. It was early summer, and the Mouse family was sitting outside, eating wild strawberries.

"Why is Wee Mouse carrying that blanket?" asked Mrs. Sparrow.

Mrs. Mouse explained that her little one was afraid of the dark. "She has terrible trouble falling asleep," said Mrs. Mouse.

"There is only one answer," said Mrs. Sparrow firmly. "When Wee Mouse goes to bed, you must sit in her room."

That night Mr. Mouse settled into a rocking chair beside Wee Mouse's bed. Wee Mouse fell asleep right away.

But when Mr. Mouse stood up to leave, Wee Mouse woke with a start.

"Don't go, Daddy!" she cried. "Stay more."

The next morning Mrs. Mouse found Mr. Mouse still sitting in the rocking chair.

"I fell asleep," said Mr. Mouse, stretching his cramped legs.

"Oh, dear," said Mrs. Mouse. "This is not the answer either."

The Mouse family grew tired and cranky. No one was getting enough sleep. One summer evening, while they were taking a stroll along the riverbank, they met old Mr. Frog.

"You all look terrible!" said the old bullfrog. "What's the matter?"

Mr. Mouse explained that they had not been sleeping well. "Wee Mouse comes and wakes us up."

"*Harrumph!*" bellowed the big frog. "There is only one answer. Lock that bad child in her room."

"Mr. Frog!" said Mrs. Mouse in a shocked voice. "That's the worst advice anyone has offered."

Mr. Mouse agreed. "Our wee mouse is not being naughty," he said. "She is afraid."

Mr. Frog just shrugged.

The next day Mr. and Mrs. Mouse decided to go see Rachel Rabbit. Rachel was wise and kind. She had raised a dozen bunnies. Surely she could help.

Wee Mouse went with her parents.

Rachel Rabbit was working in her garden. When Mr. and Mrs. Mouse told her about their problem, Rachel turned to Wee Mouse. "What is it that scares you at night?" she asked.

"The dark," said Wee Mouse. "I'm not afraid when I take my nap in the afternoon. It's not dark then. But at night Hunnible the hawk comes and hides under my bed."

"I understand," said Rachel. Then she wrote down a list of ideas to help Wee Mouse. "There's more than one answer," she said.

That evening Wee Mouse found a night-light by her bed. Mr. Mouse said she could keep it on all night. The night-light was at the top of Rachel Rabbit's list.

Before bedtime Mrs. Mouse shined a flashlight under Wee Mouse's bed. Wee Mouse looked, too.

"No one there," said Mrs. Mouse.

"No one there," said Wee Mouse.

The next day Mrs. Mouse tried another idea on Rachel Rabbit's list. She did not make Wee Mouse take a nap in the afternoon. By bedtime her little one was very tired.

During the night Wee Mouse woke up only once. Mr. and Mrs. Mouse slept soundly, too.

Wee Mouse's birthday came the next week. Her parents gave her a music box with a tiny yellow bird on top. When the music played, the canary fluttered his little wings and turned round and round.

Mr. Mouse said he was a cheery bird.

In bed that night, Wee Mouse did not ask for her special blanket. She wound up her beautiful music box again and again. Cheery Bird fluttered his soft, soft wings.

Ting. Ting-a-ling. The sound of the tinkling music lulled Wee Mouse to sleep.

She did not wake up until morning.

At breakfast, Mr. Mouse asked Wee Mouse, "Were you afraid of the dark last night?"

"No, not last night," said Wee Mouse. "Cheery Bird brought his grandfather."

Mr. and Mrs. Mouse both looked puzzled.

Wee Mouse explained. "Cheery Bird's grandfather is the king of the canaries," she said. "He's very big. He guarded me so Hunnible couldn't come. He says he will stay outside my window every night."

"Oh," said Mrs. Mouse.

"Oh, I see," said Mr. Mouse.

After that, when tree branches brushed against her window in the dark, Wee Mouse was not afraid. All she heard was the fluttering of wings, and the dark was not as dark anymore.